DATE DUE

MAR 8 1994	MAR 29 1999
DEC 4 1994	JUL 13 1999
MAR 1 1995	DEC 3
SEP 6 1995	JUN 16 2000
	DEC 18 2000
DEC 21 1995	JUN 22 2001
AUG 26 1996	APR 21 2003
NOV 5 1996	
MAR 16 1997	
JUN 9 1997	
JUL 22 1997	
FEB 17 1999 SEP 1999	

BRODART   Cat. No. 23-221

Sachiko Means Happiness

written by **Kimiko Sakai** illustrated by **Tomie Arai**

CHILDREN'S BOOK PRESS
San Francisco, California

Text copyright © 1990 by Kimiko Sakai. All rights reserved.
Illustrations copyright © 1990 by Tomie Arai. All rights reserved.
Design: Nancy Hom   Typography: Berna Alvarado-Rodriguez
Printed in Hong Kong through Interprint, Petaluma.
Children's Book Press is a nonprofit community publisher.

Publication of this book is supported in part by a grant from the
National Endowment for the Arts.

Library of Congress Cataloging-in-Publication Data
Sakai, Kimiko.
    Sachiko means happiness / written by Kimiko Sakai; illustrated by
Tomie Arai.
      p. cm.
    Summary: Although at first Sachiko is upset when her
grandmother no longer recognizes her, she grows to understand that
they can still be happy together.
    ISBN 0-89239-065-4 : $12. 95
    [1. Grandmothers—Fiction. 2. Old age—Fiction. 3. Japanese
Americans—Fiction.] I. Arai, Tomie, ill. II. Title.
PZ7. S14394Sac 1990
[E]—dc20   CIP AC

幸子

c. 1

I don't like sunsets, even if they are so beautiful. Trouble always comes in the evening. In the evening it always begins.

"Sachiko, where are you? Come and help me," called Mother.

So it began as usual.

"Here I am." I opened the door and entered the kitchen.

Mother looked at me with relief. "Sachiko, please talk with Grandmother for a while. I am busy preparing supper."

Grandmother and I have the same name, Sachiko. This name means happiness in Japanese. I was her first granddaughter. When I was born, she was very glad and gave her name to me. She loved me very much. She always looked at me lovingly and gave me special attention.

But she has changed, changed much. Now, even when I stand by her side, she does not seem to notice me.

8

"Hello, Grandma," I said to her.

She didn't look at me. She only said,
"I should go home. It's already late.
Mother will be worried."

Mother? Whose Mother is she
talking about?

"Hello, Grandma," I said again
impatiently.

She turned to me and cried angrily,
"I am not Grandmother!"

Not Grandmother? Who is she then? Why does she say she is not Grandmother? Why does she say she should go home? Why does she make so much trouble for me?

"I am Sachiko—five years old!" she said firmly.

I felt like crying. I was tired, very tired.

"Why should I take care of her?" I thought crossly. "She says she doesn't know me. Well, then I don't know her either."

As I looked at her, a wicked idea came to me. If she doesn't want to be my grandmother, she doesn't have to stay here. She can go anywhere she wants. It is her problem.

"You can go home," I said.

Her face lit up with joy.

"Do you know the way to your home?" I asked.

"Of course I know."

We went out. The air was fresh and cool and smelled of autumn.

"You are very kind," said Grandmother. "May I know your name?"

"Sachiko," I said coldly, but she didn't seem to mind.

"We have the same name. I like you very much," she said, just as if she were singing.

I didn't know where she was going, so I just followed her. When I was little she sometimes took me for a ride on her back. Her back was strong and warm then. I was her "little Sachiko" then.

We walked and walked. Suddenly, she stopped and cried, "I can't find the way. I can't!" She turned to me. She was in tears.

"What's the matter?" I asked.

"I don't know. I don't know. I can't find anything." She continued weeping.

I did not know what to do. I had never seen a grownup cry like this. I looked into her eyes trying to find the Grandmother I once knew. I saw instead a small, lost child, frightened and alone. She did not recognize anyone, not even me, and she was scared.

Slowly I began to understand. She is no longer Grandmother. She is a little girl, only five years old. But when she was five, I was not born yet. I am a stranger to her. And Mother, Father and the neighbors are strangers to her too.

"It must be very hard," I thought, "to suddenly discover that everyone is a stranger to you." I blinked back tears, but they were not tears of anger.

I looked at her for a long time. At last I hugged her and said, "Would you stay with me tonight? Surely my mother knows your house. She will call your mother and tell her you are staying with us."

She looked at me seriously and asked, "May I really stay with you?"

"Of course, you can," I answered and grasped her hand tightly to reassure her, this little five-year-old girl.

We began to walk slowly. When we got to our corner, I saw my father getting out of his car. He turned to us.

"What are you doing?" he asked.

Grandmother seemed uneasy. I patted her arm.

"Dad, this is Sachiko, my friend. Is it okay if she stays with us tonight?"

Father looked at me, and looked at Grandmother without saying anything. He nodded, "Of course, it's okay. We will be happy to have you stay with us."

Grandmother smiled at me, relieved. "Thank you," she said timidly, "Thank you."

Again Father nodded, nodded knowingly. He took my hand and Grandmother's hand. The three of us walked together towards the house.

As we walked, I turned to Grandmother. The sunset was reflected on her face.

"Look at the sunset!" I said.

We stood looking at it for a while without saying anything. It was beautiful. For the first time, I thought, I liked it.

A Note from the Author

Everybody has two grandmothers. I also did. But my grandmothers are both dead, because I am far older than you. I have been an adult for many years.

Let me tell you about one of my grandmothers, my mother's mother. She was born in 1893—long ago. Like most women of her time, her life was not easy. She was a farmer's wife and worked very hard. She had ten children and eighteen grandchildren. Two of her daughters died of illness and one of her sons died in the war. She was a good mother and grandmother—a strong, quiet woman who never complained about anything. Everybody loved her.

Soon after she turned eighty years old, she got Alzheimer's disease. This is a very sad disease. The people who get it lose most of their recent memories; they even forget who they are or what year it is. My grandmother was very kind and strong, but this disease changed her. I could not understand this disease or this change. I just kept looking at her, not knowing what to do. I was a child then. But now I am an adult and now I feel I could do something for her if she were here. That is why I wrote this story.

Kimiko Sakai

Kimiko Sakai is a librarian for the National Diet in Tokyo, Japan. When she spent a year cataloging a collection of old Japanese books at the University of California at Berkeley, she also began studying creative writing. Sakai feels a close kinship with the United States and with Asian Americans and other minorities. She lives in Tokyo, Japan and hopes to spend her yearly vacation in California. This is her first story in English.

Tomie Arai is a third generation Japanese American who was born and raised in New York City. She has spent most of the past 16 years working in New York neighborhoods as a muralist and community artist. Her work has appeared in Asian-American women's anthologies and is in the collection of the Museum of Modern Art in New York City. This is her first book for young people.